The Mirror
of the Soul

Reflection on Inner Self

Mr Ajit Kumar and Mr. Rahul Verma

Dedicated to
Almighty God

Acknowledgement

The publication of this book marks the fulfillment of a long-held dream. I am incredibly grateful to Rahul Verma, whose generous contributions were instrumental in bringing this project to life. I couldn't have done it without his firm support.

This journey would not have been possible without the grace of God and the support of my loved ones. Their encouragement and belief in me were the driving forces behind this endeavor.

I am deeply grateful to God for providing me with the strength and inspiration to overcome the challenges I faced during the writing process. My heartfelt thanks go to my parents, whose constant support and late-night refreshments fueled my efforts. My brother and Sister in law's constant encouragement and belief in me were invaluable.

I am indebted to Himanshu for creating the book's stunning cover page and to Manjay for meticulously proofreading the entire manuscript. I deeply appreciate their dedication and willingness to contribute their time and expertise to this project, despite their busy schedules.

I would also like to express my sincere gratitude to Rashmi Gosain, whose insightful suggestions sparked many of the ideas within these pages. My academic mentors, Dr. Nibedita Hazarika and Dr. Rashee Singh (HOD), have consistently believed in me and encouraged me to reach my full potential. I am also grateful for the stanch support of Dr. Savita Sharma, Abhishek Mehra, Vrinda Goel, Vishesh Thakur and librarian Ms. Mamta Srivastava.

I am grateful to Gunjan Kadaria and Sunil Navale for patiently listening to my stories and offering their valuable insights. A special thanks to my lifelong friends – Surbhi, Prashant, Sunita, Nishi, Shivam, Azazul, Simrat, Somya, Pawan and Khuloos – for their enormous support throughout my journey. I am also grateful to my school friends, Sarita Sonkhla and Abhishek Bhalla, whose insights indirectly inspired many of the ideas presented in this book.

Finally, I acknowledge the countless others whose contributions, though unmentioned, are deeply appreciated. I understand that every contribution, no matter how small, played a significant role in the creation of this book.knowledge original image creaters who allows us to use their artistic work to add value in our art work.

Index

Chapter 01

Writing and the Construction of Reality

The pen, a seemingly simple instrument, holds within it the power to shape not just words on a page, but the very essence of our being. It is a conduit for the inner self, a tool for self-expression, and a testament to the enduring human desire to leave a mark on the world.

From the earliest cave paintings to the intricate calligraphy of ancient civilizations, the pen has been an indispensable companion on humanity's journey of self-discovery. It has been used to record history, to share knowledge, to weave tales of love and loss, and to articulate the deepest of human emotions.

For the writer, the pen is more than just an object; it is an extension of their soul. It is the vessel through which thoughts and feelings flow, transforming into tangible expressions of the inner self. The act of writing, the deliberate placement of ink on paper, is a deeply personal and intimate process. It requires introspection, vulnerability, and a willingness to confront one's own thoughts and emotions.

Through the act of writing, we begin to understand ourselves better. We explore the nuances of our own minds, delve into the depths of our desires and fears, and confront the contradictions that lie within us. The pen becomes a mirror, reflecting back to us the complexities of our own being.

The process of writing can be both exhilarating and daunting. It can be a source of immense joy and fulfillment, as we bring our inner world to life on the page. But it can also be a source of anxiety and self-doubt, as we grapple with the fear of judgment and the pressure to express ourselves authentically.

However, it is precisely this vulnerability that allows for true self-expression. When we dare to put our thoughts and feelings into words, we open ourselves up to the possibility of genuine connection with others. We share our stories, our hopes, our dreams, and in doing so, we create a sense of shared humanity.

The pen, therefore, is not merely a tool for communication; it is a tool for self-discovery and connection. It allows us to bridge the gap between our inner and outer worlds, to make sense of our experiences, and to find meaning in the human condition.

In a world that often values speed and efficiency above all else, the act of writing offers a much-needed respite. It allows us to slow down, to reflect, and to connect with the deeper currents of our being. It encourages us to embrace the power of introspection and to cultivate a deeper understanding of ourselves and the world around us.

So, let us cherish the pen, not just as a tool for writing, but as a tool for self-discovery. Let us use it to explore the depths of our own souls, to share our stories with the world, and to leave a lasting legacy of our own unique perspective. For in the act of writing, we not only shape the world around us, but we also shape ourselves.

Chapter 02

Footprints on the Soul

The humble stair, often overlooked in the grand scheme of architectural design, offers a profound metaphor for the human journey. It is a constant, ever-present reminder of the ascent, the descent, the forward and backward movement that characterizes our lives. Each step, a microcosm of progress and regression, joy and sorrow, struggle and triumph.

Climbing stairs demands effort. It requires the expenditure of physical energy, a conscious decision to move upwards, to overcome gravity and reach a higher point.This mirrors the challenges we face in life – the need to push ourselves beyond our comfort zones, to strive for personal growth, to achieve our goals. Each step taken, each obstacle overcome, strengthens our resolve and builds our character.

But the journey is not always linear. We may stumble, lose our footing, and even fall. We may encounter unexpected obstacles, encounter unforeseen detours, or simply need to rest. These setbacks, like the occasional misstep on the stairs, are inevitable. They are opportunities for reflection, for reassessment, for learning and growth.

Descending the stairs can be just as meaningful as ascending. It can represent a period of introspection, a time for contemplation and rejuvenation. It can be a time to release the burdens of the day, to let go of anxieties and worries, and to simply be present in the moment.

The stairs also symbolize the cyclical nature of life. We are constantly in motion, moving through phases of growth and decline, of achievement and rest. We experience periods of ascent, reaching new heights and expanding our horizons, followed by periods of descent, where we reflect, regroup, and prepare for the next phase of our journey.

Furthermore, the stairs can represent the interconnectedness of our lives. Each step we take, whether ascending or descending, affects those around us. Our actions, our choices, have a ripple effect, influencing the lives of others in both positive and negative ways.

Ultimately, the stairs serve as a powerful reminder of the human condition. They are a metaphor for the journey of life, with its inherent challenges, triumphs, and cyclical nature. They remind us of the importance of perseverance, resilience, and the constant striving for personal growth.

So, the next time you encounter a set of stairs, take a moment to reflect. Consider the journey you are on, the challenges you face, and the progress you have made. Acknowledge the inevitable setbacks and the importance of rest and reflection. And remember that even in the face of adversity, you have the strength and resilience to climb higher, to reach new heights, and to continue on your unique and ever-evolving journey.

Chapter 03

The Whispers of the Fur: Insights into the Human Condition

The bond between a pet and their human companion is a unique and often profound one. Pets, whether furry, feathered, or scaled, have the remarkable ability to mirror aspects of our own selves and enrich our lives in ways we may not fully realize.

One of the most significant ways pets impact our lives is through their unconditional love. Unlike human relationships that can be complex and fraught with expectations, a pet's love is pure and unwavering. Their joy at our return, their gentle companionship, and their unwavering loyalty can provide a sense of comfort and security that can be invaluable in a world that often feels chaotic and uncertain.

Furthermore, pets encourage us to live in the present moment. Their playful antics, their curiosity about the world, and their simple pleasures remind us to slow down, appreciate the small things, and find joy in the everyday. They help us shed the burdens of the past and the anxieties of the future, allowing us to embrace the present with a renewed sense of wonder and appreciation.

Pets also play a vital role in fostering a sense of responsibility and empathy within us.Caring for another living being requires dedication, patience, and a deep sense of compassion. Feeding them, grooming them, and ensuring their well-being instills a sense of duty and responsibility that can translate into other areas of our lives. Moreover, witnessing a pet's vulnerability and their dependence on us can cultivate empathy and a deeper understanding of the needs of others.

In addition to their emotional benefits, pets can also have a positive impact on our physical health. Studies have shown that pet ownership can lower blood pressure, reduce stress levels, and even improve cardiovascular health. The simple act of petting an animal can release endorphins, natural mood boosters that promote feelings of well-being and happiness.

However, the relationship between a pet and their human is a two-way street. Just as pets enrich our lives, we also have a responsibility to care for them and provide them with a loving and nurturing environment. This includes ensuring their physical and emotional well-being, providing them with adequate exercise and mental stimulation, and seeking veterinary care when needed.

In conclusion, the bond between a pet and their human is a unique and enriching one. Pets offer unconditional love, encourage us to live in the present moment, and foster a sense of responsibility and empathy within us. In return, we have a responsibility to provide them with a loving and nurturing home, ensuring their well-being and happiness. The relationship between a pet and their human is a testament to the power of love, companionship, and the profound connection we can share with other living beings.

Chapter 04

The Unraveling and Reweaving of Self: A Journey of Transformation

The humble thread, often overlooked in the grand tapestry of our lives, holds within it a remarkable metaphor for the intricate nature of our being. It is a delicate yet resilient strand, connecting, binding, and weaving the various facets of our existence into a unique and intricate pattern.

Just as a thread is woven into fabric, our experiences, thoughts, emotions, and relationships intertwine to create the fabric of our lives. Each memory, each interaction, each joy and sorrow, becomes a thread woven into the tapestry of our being. These threads, seemingly insignificant on their own, combine to form the intricate patterns that define who we are.

The strength of a thread lies in its ability to connect. It binds together disparate elements, creating a cohesive whole. Similarly, our relationships, both personal and professional, connect us to others, forming a network of support and interdependence. These connections, like the threads in a woven fabric, provide strength and resilience, enabling us to navigate the challenges and triumphs of life.

The thread also symbolizes the continuous and evolving nature of our being. Just as a thread can be lengthened, shortened, or woven into different patterns, our selves are constantly in a state of flux. We are constantly growing, learning, and evolving, adapting to new experiences and navigating the ever-changing landscape of life.

Furthermore, the thread can represent the delicate balance between fragility and resilience. While seemingly fragile, a thread can be remarkably strong when woven into a larger structure. Similarly, we may experience moments of vulnerability and fragility, but within us lies an inherent resilience, an ability to withstand challenges and emerge stronger.

The thread also serves as a reminder of the interconnectedness of all things. Just as a single thread contributes to the overall integrity of the fabric, our individual actions and choices have a ripple effect, influencing the lives of others and shaping the collective human experience.

In conclusion, the thread, in its simplicity, offers a profound metaphor for the intricate nature of our being. It symbolizes the interconnectedness of our experiences, the strength of our relationships, the continuous evolution of ourselves, and the delicate balance between fragility and resilience. By recognizing the thread within ourselves and understanding its significance, we can gain a deeper appreciation for the intricate tapestry of our lives and the profound connections we share with others.

Chapter 05

The Bookworm's Odyssey: Exploring the Self Through Literature

The book, a seemingly simple object, holds within it the power to transport us to other worlds, to introduce us to new ideas, and to illuminate the depths of the human experience. But beyond mere entertainment, books offer a unique and profound pathway to self-discovery.

Reading allows us to step into the shoes of others, to experience their joys and sorrows, their triumphs and failures. Through the stories we encounter, we gain empathy, understanding, and a broader perspective on the human condition. We learn to appreciate the diversity of human experience, to recognize the commonalities that bind us together, and to cultivate compassion for those who are different from ourselves.

Books also serve as a mirror, reflecting back to us our own thoughts, feelings, and experiences. In the characters we encounter, we may recognize aspects of ourselves, both the good and the bad. We may confront our own fears, anxieties, and desires, and gain a deeper understanding of our own motivations and behaviors.

Furthermore, books provide a safe space for introspection and self-reflection. They offer a quiet refuge from the distractions of daily life, allowing us to delve into our own inner worlds and explore the complexities of our own minds. Through reading, we can confront our own biases, challenge our assumptions, and cultivate a deeper understanding of ourselves and the world around us.

Books also offer a unique opportunity for personal growth.[9] They expose us to new ideas, challenge our existing beliefs, and broaden our horizons. They introduce us to different cultures, different perspectives, and different ways of thinking, expanding our understanding of the world and our place within it.

Moreover, reading can be a powerful tool for personal development. By immersing ourselves in the lives and experiences of others, we can gain valuable insights into human behavior, develop our critical thinking skills, and enhance our communication and emotional intelligence.

In conclusion, books offer a unique and profound pathway to self-discovery. They allow us to step into the shoes of others, to confront our own inner selves, and to cultivate a deeper understanding of the world around us. Through reading, we can expand our horizons, cultivate empathy, and embark on a lifelong journey of personal growth and self-discovery.

Chapter 06

The Psychology of Hue

Colours, seemingly simple elements of our visual world, hold a profound and often overlooked connection to our inner selves. They are more than just visual stimuli; they evoke emotions, trigger memories, and shape our perceptions of the world around us.

From the moment we are born, colours begin to influence our experiences. The vibrant hues of childhood toys, the soothing blues of the sky, the fiery reds of a sunset – these colours become woven into the fabric of our memories and emotions.

Our preferences for certain colours often reflect deep-seated personality traits. People who gravitate towards bold, vibrant colours like red and orange are often perceived as energetic, passionate, and confident. Those who favor calming hues like blue and green may be seen as peaceful, introspective, and in tune with nature.

Colour can also be a powerful tool for self-expression. Artists, designers, and even fashion enthusiasts use colour to communicate their unique personalities and emotions. The vibrant colours of an abstract painting can convey a sense of joy and exuberance, while the muted tones of a minimalist design can evoke feelings of tranquility and serenity.

Furthermore, colour therapy, a form of alternative medicine, explores the therapeutic potential of colour. It is believed that different colours can have a profound impact on our physical and emotional well-being. For example, red is often associated with increased energy and stimulation, while blue is believed to have a calming and soothing effect.

Beyond their personal significance, colours also play a crucial role in shaping our social and cultural experiences. Different colours hold different meanings in different cultures. For example, white is associated with purity and innocence in many Western cultures, while in some Eastern cultures, it symbolizes mourning.

In conclusion, colours are more than just visual sensations; they are deeply intertwined with our inner selves. They evoke emotions, trigger memories, and influence our perceptions of the world. By understanding the impact of colours on our lives, we can gain a deeper appreciation for the nuances of our own experiences and the rich tapestry of human emotion

Chapter 07

The Deck of Being: A Metaphor for the Human Experience

The humble playing card, often associated with leisure and entertainment, holds within it a surprising depth of meaning when viewed through the lens of self-reflection.

The deck itself, with its 52 cards, each unique in its suit and value, can be seen as a microcosm of human experience. The four suits – hearts, diamonds, spades, and clubs – represent the diverse aspects of our being: love, passion, intellect, and duty. Each card within a suit, from the lowly two to the powerful ace, symbolizes the varying degrees of these qualities within us.

The act of shuffling the deck mirrors the unpredictable and ever-changing nature of life. Just as the cards are randomly mixed, our lives are filled with unexpected twists and turns, moments of joy and sorrow, triumphs and setbacks. The shuffle represents the uncertainty of the future, the constant state of flux that characterizes our existence.

Drawing a card from the shuffled deck can be seen as a moment of introspection. Each card drawn offers a glimpse into the subconscious, a reflection of our current state of mind. The heart may symbolize a need for love and connection, the spade may indicate a period of introspection and contemplation, while the diamond may signify a time of opportunity and growth.

Playing card games, whether it's a simple game of solitaire or a complex game of poker, requires strategic thinking, decision-making, and risk-taking. These skills, honed through card games, translate to real-life situations. We learn to assess situations, weigh the potential outcomes of our actions, and make calculated risks.

Furthermore, card games often involve social interaction and communication. They provide opportunities for connection, competition, and collaboration. These interactions, whether cooperative or competitive, reflect the dynamics of human relationships, teaching us about cooperation, negotiation, and sportsmanship.

In conclusion, the seemingly frivolous act of playing cards offers a profound metaphor for the human experience. The deck, with its diverse cards and unpredictable nature, mirrors the complexities of life. The act of playing, with its strategic thinking, decision-making, and social interactions, reflects the challenges and joys of human existence. Through the lens of a deck of cards, we can gain valuable insights into ourselves, our relationships, and the unpredictable nature of life itself.

Chapter 08

The Bed as Refuge: Finding Solace in Sleep

The mattress, a seemingly mundane object, holds a profound significance in our lives. It is more than just a piece of furniture; it is a sanctuary, a place of rest, and a reflection of our individual needs and desires.

The choice of mattress itself is a deeply personal one. Factors such as comfort, support, and even aesthetics play a crucial role in our selection. We seek a mattress that will provide us with the optimal level of support for our bodies, ensuring a restful and rejuvenating sleep. This personalized choice reflects our individual needs and preferences, highlighting the unique characteristics of each individual.

The mattress also serves as a microcosm of our inner world. It is a space of retreat, a place where we can escape the stresses and anxieties of daily life and simply be. As we lie on the mattress, we shed the burdens of the day, allowing our minds and bodies to relax and rejuvenate. It is in this space of quietude that we often find ourselves reflecting on our thoughts, feelings, and experiences.

Furthermore, the quality of our sleep, significantly influenced by the comfort of our mattress, has a profound impact on our overall well-being. A good night's sleep is essential for physical and mental health. It allows our bodies to repair and rejuvenate, improves cognitive function, and boosts our mood.

The mattress also symbolizes the importance of self-care. It is a reminder that we need to prioritize our physical and mental well-being. Just as we invest in a comfortable and supportive mattress, we need to invest in ourselves, ensuring that we have the necessary resources and support to thrive. This includes prioritizing rest, relaxation, and activities that nourish our minds and bodies.

In conclusion, the mattress, though seemingly mundane, holds a profound significance in our lives. It is a reflection of our individual needs and desires, a sanctuary for rest and rejuvenation, and a symbol of the importance of self-care. By investing in a comfortable and supportive mattress, we are investing in our own well-being, ensuring that we have the foundation for a healthy and fulfilling life.

Chapter 09

Quenching the Flames

The fire extinguisher, a seemingly simple device, offers a profound metaphor for the human experience. It represents our capacity to extinguish the fires within ourselves – the anxieties, fears, and negative emotions that can consume us if left unchecked.

Just as a fire extinguisher is designed to quickly and effectively suppress flames, we must develop the inner resources to extinguish the fires within. These fires can manifest in various forms: uncontrolled anger, crippling anxiety, destructive self-criticism, and debilitating fear.

One of the key components of a fire extinguisher is its pressurized agent, which propels the extinguishing substance towards the fire. Similarly, we need to cultivate inner strength and resilience, the "pressurized agent" within ourselves. This inner strength comes from practices like mindfulness, meditation, and cultivating self-compassion. These practices help us to become more aware of our emotions, to understand their triggers, and to develop the capacity to respond to them in a calm and mindful way.

Furthermore, the fire extinguisher requires proper maintenance and regular inspection to ensure its effectiveness. Similarly, we must regularly tend to our inner well-being. This involves practices such as healthy eating, regular exercise, and sufficient sleep. These practices nourish our bodies and minds, enabling us to effectively extinguish the fires that arise within.

The fire extinguisher also symbolizes the importance of preparedness. Just as a fire extinguisher is readily available in case of an emergency, we must cultivate the inner resources necessary to effectively manage our emotions and respond to challenges with grace and resilience. This involves developing coping mechanisms, building strong support networks, and learning to recognize the early warning signs of emotional distress.

Finally, the fire extinguisher serves as a reminder that we are not powerless in the face of emotional turmoil. Just as a fire extinguisher can quickly and effectively suppress flames, we have the capacity to extinguish the fires within ourselves. By cultivating inner strength, practicing self-care, and developing effective coping mechanisms, we can create a more peaceful and fulfilling inner landscape.

Chapter 10

The Self in Motion: Exploring Ourselves Through Travel

The humble objects we use for transport – the car, the bicycle, the airplane, the train – offer profound metaphors for the journey of self-discovery. Each mode of transport reflects a unique facet of our inner landscape, our aspirations, and our approach to life.

The car, with its powerful engine and comfortable interior, can symbolize ambition and a desire for control. It represents our drive to reach our destinations quickly and efficiently, often prioritizing speed and convenience. However, the car can also symbolize a sense of isolation, separating us from the immediate environment and hindering genuine connection with the world around us.

The bicycle, in contrast, represents a more grounded and deliberate approach to life. It requires effort and engagement, demanding that we actively participate in the journey. Cycling allows us to connect with our surroundings, to experience the world more intimately and to appreciate the nuances of the landscape. It symbolizes a slower, more mindful approach to life, emphasizing the journey itself rather than solely the destination.

The airplane, with its ability to soar above the clouds, symbolizes our aspirations for freedom and our desire to escape the constraints of the everyday. It represents our yearning for adventure, for new horizons, and for a broader perspective on the world. However, the airplane can also symbolize a sense of detachment, a feeling of being removed from the ground, disconnected from the realities of daily life.

The train, with its steady rhythm and predetermined route, symbolizes the passage of time, the inevitability of change, and the interconnectedness of all things. It represents a journey that unfolds gradually, allowing for reflection and contemplation. The train can also symbolize the importance of community and the shared experience of the journey.

Each mode of transport, therefore, offers a unique perspective on the human condition. They reflect our aspirations, our fears, our desires for freedom and connection, and our approaches to navigating the journey of life. By examining our preferences for different modes of transport, we can gain valuable insights into our own inner landscapes and the ways in which we navigate the world around us

Chapter 11

The Cracks in the Facade: Exploring the Vulnerabilities Beneath

The seemingly mundane false ceiling, a layer of concealment covering the true structure above, offers a surprisingly potent metaphor for the human experience. It speaks to our inherent need to construct, conceal, and present a curated version of ourselves to the world.

Just as a false ceiling hides the complexities of the original structure, we often present a carefully crafted facade to the world. We conceal our vulnerabilities, insecurities, and inner turmoil beneath a polished exterior, striving to project an image of confidence and composure. This facade, like the false ceiling, can serve a protective function, shielding us from judgment and criticism.

However, much like a poorly constructed false ceiling that can conceal underlying problems, this facade can also become a barrier to genuine connection and self-growth. It can prevent us from authentically expressing ourselves, from seeking help when we need it, and from truly connecting with others on a deeper level.

The process of constructing a false ceiling involves careful planning and execution. Similarly, we invest considerable effort in constructing and maintaining our self-image. We choose our words carefully, curate our online presence, and strive to present a version of ourselves that aligns with our desired self-perception. This constant effort to maintain appearances can be exhausting and ultimately inauthentic.

Furthermore, the false ceiling, while concealing the original structure, can also enhance the aesthetics of a space. Similarly, our carefully constructed facades can serve to enhance our self-esteem and confidence. By presenting ourselves in a positive light, we can boost our self-image and cultivate a sense of self-worth.

Ultimately, the false ceiling serves as a reminder of the complexities of human identity. It highlights the tension between our authentic selves and the curated versions we present to the world. By recognizing the role of the "false ceiling" in our own lives, we can begin to explore the underlying structures of our being, embrace our vulnerabilities, and cultivate a more authentic and fulfilling sense of self.

Chapter 12

A Step in the Right Direction

The humble shoe, often taken for granted, offers a surprisingly profound reflection of the self. More than just a utilitarian object, shoes embody our aspirations, our insecurities, and the way we navigate the world.

The choice of footwear is deeply personal. From the rugged hiking boots of the adventurer to the sleek stilettos of the confident executive, our shoes reflect our lifestyle, our personality, and the image we wish to project. They are an extension of our identity, a silent statement about who we are and who we want to be.

The act of putting on shoes can be seen as a ritual of preparation, a symbolic act of stepping into the world. It is a moment of transition, a conscious decision to engage with the outside world. The feeling of stepping into comfortable, well-fitting shoes can provide a sense of security and confidence, empowering us to face the challenges that lie ahead.

Conversely, uncomfortable or ill-fitting shoes can hinder our progress and dampen our spirits. They can cause physical discomfort, distract us from our goals, and even impact our mood. Similarly, self-doubt, insecurities, and negative self-talk can weigh us down, hindering our progress and preventing us from reaching our full potential.

The way we walk in our shoes also reveals much about our inner state. A confident stride reflects a sense of purpose and self-assurance, while a hesitant gait may betray underlying anxieties. Our shoes, in a sense, guide our steps, shaping our movement and influencing our interactions with the world around us.

Furthermore, the care we take with our shoes reflects our overall approach to life. Those who meticulously care for their footwear, polishing them regularly and ensuring they are always in good condition, often demonstrate a similar level of care for themselves and their possessions.

In conclusion, the humble shoe, though often overlooked, offers a profound reflection of the self. It embodies our aspirations, our insecurities, and the way we navigate the world. By paying attention to our footwear choices and the way we interact with them, we can gain valuable insights into our own inner landscape and the journey we are on.

Chapter 13

The Chair as Metaphor: Exploring the Human Condition Through Sitting

The humble chair, often taken for granted as a mere piece of furniture, offers a surprisingly profound reflection of the human experience. It is a place of rest, a symbol of authority, and a reflection of our individual needs and desires.

The act of sitting itself is a fundamental human experience. It represents a moment of pause, a time for reflection and contemplation. It allows us to withdraw from the demands of the external world and turn inward, to connect with our inner selves.

The type of chair we choose to sit in often reflects our personality and our social status. The executive chair, with its plush leather and commanding presence, symbolizes power and authority. The comfortable armchair, with its soft cushions and inviting embrace, reflects a desire for comfort and relaxation. The simple folding chair, on the other hand, can symbolize humility, simplicity, and a willingness to adapt to different situations.

The chair also plays a significant role in social interactions. It defines our roles and relationships within a given space. The chair at the head of the table signifies leadership, while the chairs arranged in a circle promote equality and inclusivity. The act of offering someone a seat can be a gesture of hospitality and respect, while being denied a seat can be a subtle form of exclusion.

Furthermore, the chair can be a symbol of our individual journeys. It represents the various stages of life, from the high chair of infancy to the rocking chair of old age. Each chair we encounter along the way reflects our changing needs and evolving perspectives.

In conclusion, the chair, though seemingly mundane, offers a profound reflection of the human experience. It is a place of rest, a symbol of status and power, and a reflection of our individual needs and desires. By examining our relationship with chairs, we can gain valuable insights into our own inner landscapes and the ways in which we navigate the social and physical world around us.

Chapter 14

Finding Our Place in Time

The calendar, a seemingly mundane object used to track the passage of time, offers a surprisingly profound reflection of the human experience. It is a constant reminder of our mortality, a framework for our lives, and a tool for both planning and reflecting on our journey.

The act of marking dates on a calendar – birthdays, anniversaries, deadlines, appointments – signifies our attempt to exert control over time, to impose order on the unpredictable flow of existence. We strive to plan and organize our lives, to make the most of our time, and to achieve our goals within a specific timeframe.

The calendar also serves as a constant reminder of our mortality. The ticking clock, the changing dates, the inexorable march of time – these all serve as reminders of our own finiteness. This awareness can be both daunting and motivating. It can motivate us to make the most of our time, to pursue our passions, and to live a meaningful life.

Furthermore, the calendar provides a framework for our lives. It divides time into discrete units – days, weeks, months, years – providing a sense of structure and predictability. This structure can be both comforting and confining. It can provide a sense of stability and security, while also limiting our spontaneity and restricting our ability to fully embrace the present moment.

The calendar also serves as a tool for reflection. By reviewing past events, we can learn from our mistakes, celebrate our successes, and gain a deeper understanding of our own growth and development. We can identify patterns in our behavior, recognize recurring themes in our lives, and make informed decisions about our future.

In conclusion, the calendar, though seemingly mundane, offers a profound reflection of the human experience. It is a reminder of our mortality, a framework for our lives, and a tool for both planning and reflection. By understanding the significance of the calendar, we can gain a deeper appreciation for the preciousness of time and make conscious choices about how we spend our days.

Chapter 15

The Edge of Existence

The humble scissor, a seemingly simple tool, offers a surprising depth of metaphor for the human experience. It is an instrument of both creation and destruction, a symbol of control and vulnerability, and a reflection of our capacity for both precision and chaos.

The act of cutting, whether it's trimming a hedge, snipping a piece of fabric, or simply opening a package, requires a delicate balance of force and control. It demands precision and intention, a careful consideration of the desired outcome. This mirrors the challenges we face in navigating our own lives. We must carefully consider our actions, weigh the potential consequences, and strive for a balance between decisiveness and restraint.

The scissor also symbolizes the power of transformation. It can be used to reshape, to redefine, to bring something new into existence. Just as the scissor transforms raw materials into something new and useful, we too have the capacity to transform ourselves. We can shed old habits, overcome challenges, and cultivate new skills and perspectives.

However, the scissor can also be a tool of destruction. A careless cut can ruin a piece of fabric, damage a valuable object, or even cause injury. Similarly, our words and actions, if not carefully considered, can have unintended consequences. We must be mindful of the potential impact of our choices and strive to use our power wisely and responsibly.

The scissor also represents the delicate balance between control and vulnerability. While we wield the scissor, we are also vulnerable to its sharp edges. We must be mindful of our own power and the potential for unintended consequences. This reflects the inherent vulnerability of the human condition. We are both creators and potential destroyers, both powerful and vulnerable.

In conclusion, the scissor, though seemingly mundane, offers a profound metaphor for the human experience. It symbolizes our capacity for creation and destruction, our need for control and our vulnerability to unintended consequences. By understanding the symbolism of the scissor, we can gain a deeper appreciation for the delicate balance of power and responsibility that characterizes the human condition.

Chapter 16

The Art of Self-Adornment

Jewelry, more than mere adornment, often serves as a powerful reflection of our inner selves. It's a form of visual storytelling, a way to express our unique personalities, beliefs, and experiences. From the delicate shimmer of a silver pendant to the bold sparkle of a diamond necklace, each piece holds a unique resonance, connecting us to our past, present, and future.

For many, jewelry transcends the physical. It becomes an extension of their identity, a symbol of their journey. A family heirloom, passed down through generations, carries the weight of history, a tangible link to ancestors and their legacies. It whispers stories of love, loss, and resilience, reminding us of our roots and the enduring power of family bonds.

Similarly, jewelry can mark significant milestones. An engagement ring symbolizes a promise of eternal love, a graduation necklace commemorates a hard-earned achievement, or a birthstone bracelet celebrates the arrival of a new life. These pieces become cherished reminders of pivotal moments, encapsulating joy, hope, and the passage of time.

Beyond sentimental value, jewelry can also be a powerful tool for self-expression. It allows us to showcase our individuality, to project the image we wish to portray to the world. A minimalist aesthetic might reflect a preference for simplicity and understated elegance, while a bohemian style could suggest a free-spirited and adventurous nature. Bold, vibrant colors might signify a playful and exuberant personality, while classic designs could speak to a timeless sense of sophistication.

Jewelry can also be a form of self-care. The act of choosing and wearing jewelry can be a mindful experience. It allows us to pause, to appreciate the beauty of the piece, and to connect with the emotions it evokes. Whether it's the cool touch of silver against the skin or the warm glow of gold, wearing jewelry can be a comforting and grounding experience, a small act of self-love and appreciation.

Furthermore, jewelry can be a source of empowerment and confidence. A statement necklace can add a touch of boldness to an outfit, while a pair of sparkling earrings can elevate one's mood. Wearing jewelry that makes us feel good about ourselves can have a profound impact on our self-perception and how we interact with the world.

However, the relationship between jewelry and self is not always straightforward. The pressure to conform to societal expectations or to acquire expensive pieces can sometimes overshadow the genuine joy of personal expression. It's important to remember that true value lies not in the monetary worth of the jewelry, but in the personal significance it holds.

Ultimately, jewelry is a deeply personal and multifaceted aspect of human expression. It's a reflection of our unique journeys, our deepest values, and the stories we wish to tell. Whether it's a cherished heirloom, a symbol of a momentous occasion or simply a piece that brings us joy, jewelry allows us to connect with ourselves and the world in a unique and meaningful way.

Chapter 17

The Instrument as Mirror: Reflecting on Self

The relationship between a musical instrument and the self is a profound one, extending far beyond mere entertainment. It's a journey of self-discovery, a form of expression, and a means of cultivating inner peace and resilience.

Learning to play an instrument demands dedication and perseverance. The initial struggles, the frustration of not hitting the right notes or mastering a difficult passage, can be challenging. Yet, overcoming these obstacles instills a sense of accomplishment and a belief in one's own capabilities. This process of learning and growing parallels the challenges we face in life, teaching us valuable lessons about resilience, patience, and the importance of perseverance.

Music, as an art form, provides a unique avenue for self-expression. It allows us to translate our emotions, thoughts, and experiences into tangible sounds. Whether it's the melancholic melody of a blues guitar or the joyful exuberance of a jazz trumpet, music offers a language that transcends words, enabling us to communicate our innermost selves in a powerful and authentic way.

Playing an instrument can also be a meditative practice, fostering a sense of calm and inner peace. The act of focusing on the music, on the intricate interplay of notes and rhythms, can quiet the mind and alleviate stress. It provides a sanctuary where worries and anxieties can be temporarily forgotten, allowing us to connect with ourselves on a deeper level.

Furthermore, the social aspect of music cannot be overlooked. Playing in a band or orchestra fosters a sense of community and belonging. It teaches us the importance of collaboration, communication, and mutual respect. Through shared musical experiences, we learn to appreciate the diverse talents and perspectives of others, broadening our understanding of the world around us.

In conclusion, the relationship between a musical instrument and the self is a multifaceted one. It's a journey of personal growth, a form of self-expression, a source of inner peace, and a means of connecting with others. Whether we're playing for ourselves or sharing our music with the world, the instrument becomes an extension of our being, a reflection of our unique spirit and soul.

Chapter 18

Beading Peace

Mala beads, traditionally used in Buddhist and Hindu practices, offer more than just religious significance. They serve as powerful tools for personal growth, mindfulness, and inner peace. These strings of beads often made from natural materials like wood, seeds, or gemstones, act as physical reminders to stay present and cultivate inner tranquility.

The act of holding and manipulating the mala beads during meditation or prayer can be deeply grounding. The rhythmic counting of each bead helps to quiet the mind, bringing focus away from distracting thoughts and anxieties. This repetitive motion can induce a meditative state, allowing for deeper introspection and a greater sense of inner peace.

Furthermore, mala beads can be used as a form of mindfulness in everyday life. By consciously engaging with the beads throughout the day, such as by gently stroking them or simply holding them in your hand, you can cultivate a sense of present moment awareness. This can help to reduce stress, increase focus, and foster a greater sense of calm and well-being.

The choice of beads themselves can also hold personal significance. Different gemstones are believed to possess unique healing properties. For example, amethyst is often associated with tranquility and spiritual awareness, while carnelian is thought to enhance creativity and courage. By selecting beads that resonate with your personal needs and intentions, you can create a mala that is uniquely meaningful and supportive of your spiritual journey.

Beyond their practical applications, mala beads can also serve as powerful symbols of personal growth and transformation. Each bead can represent a step on the path to enlightenment, a reminder of the progress made and the journey still to be undertaken. The act of creating your own mala can be a deeply meaningful and empowering experience, allowing you to infuse each bead with your own intentions and aspirations.

In conclusion, mala beads offer a multifaceted approach to personal growth and well-being. They serve as tools for meditation, mindfulness, and self-reflection, helping to cultivate inner peace and reduce stress. Whether used for religious purposes or simply as aids for personal development, mala beads can be powerful allies on the journey of self-discovery and spiritual awakening.

Chapter 19

Aromatic Awakening: Incense and the Inner Journey

The incense stick, is often overlooked as a simple aromatic offering, holds a profound connection to the self. Beyond its fragrant properties, it serves as a powerful tool for meditation, relaxation, and spiritual connection.

The act of lighting an incense stick is a ritual in itself. The gentle flame, flickering to life, symbolizes the awakening of consciousness. The rising smoke, carrying the fragrant essence, can be seen as a representation of our thoughts and aspirations ascending towards higher realms. This simple act can be a powerful way to transition from the mundane to the meditative, creating a sacred space for inner reflection.

The fragrance of the incense itself plays a significant role in its impact on the self. Different scents are believed to have unique therapeutic properties. For example, lavender is often associated with relaxation and stress relief, while sandalwood is thought to promote calmness and spiritual awareness. By choosing incense that resonates with your current needs and intentions, you can create an aromatic environment that supports your inner journey.

The act of observing the incense stick burning can also be a form of mindfulness. The gentle sway of the smoke, the subtle changes in the intensity of the fragrance and the gradual shortening of the stick all serve as reminders to stay present in the moment. This focus on the present experience can help to quiet the mind, reduce anxiety, and cultivate a deeper sense of inner peace.

Furthermore, the use of incense can be a significant part of spiritual practices. In many cultures, incense is used to create a sacred atmosphere for prayer, meditation, and ritual. The fragrant smoke is believed to purify the environment and elevate the spirit, creating a conducive atmosphere for connecting with the divine.

In conclusion, the incense stick, seemingly simple and insignificant, holds a profound connection to the self. It serves as a tool for meditation, relaxation, and spiritual connection, offering a pathway to inner peace and self-discovery. By consciously engaging with the act of lighting and observing the incense, we can cultivate a deeper awareness of the present moment and connect with our inner selves on a more profound level.

Chapter 20

Celebrating Individuality through Headwear

The humble hat, often seen as a mere accessory, can hold a surprisingly profound connection to the self. Beyond simply shielding us from the sun or rain, it can be a powerful symbol of identity, a reflection of personal style, and even a tool for self-expression.

For many, the choice of hat is deeply personal. A wide-brimmed straw hat might evoke images of carefree summer days and leisurely strolls along the beach, while a sleek fedora might suggest a more sophisticated and mysterious persona. A baseball cap can signify a love for a particular team or a connection to a specific subculture, while a colorful beanie can express individuality and a playful spirit.

Beyond its aesthetic function, the hat can also serve as a form of self-protection. It can shield us not only from the elements but also from the scrutiny of others, providing a sense of anonymity and allowing us to step outside of our usual roles. This can be particularly liberating for those who crave a sense of privacy or simply enjoy the freedom of being unrecognized.

For some, the hat becomes an integral part of their identity, a visual marker that sets them apart from the crowd. A signature style, such as a stetson worn by a cowboy or a beret favored by an artist, can become synonymous with the individual, creating a lasting impression and contributing to their public image.

Furthermore, the act of wearing a hat can be a form of self-care. It can provide a sense of comfort and security, a familiar touch that grounds us and provides a sense of stability. For some, the simple act of putting on a hat can be a ritual, a way to prepare for the day ahead or to transition from one state of mind to another.

In conclusion, the hat, though seemingly insignificant, can hold a surprisingly profound connection to the self. It is more than just a head covering; it is a reflection of our personality, a tool for self-expression, and a symbol of our individuality. Whether it's a simple beanie or an elaborately decorated fedora, the hat we choose to wear tells a story about who we are and how we wish to present ourselves to the world.

Chapter 21

Deciphering the Ring: Symbols of Self

The ring, a seemingly simple piece of jewelry, holds a profound connection to the self. Beyond its aesthetic appeal, it serves as a powerful symbol, a marker of milestones, and a reflection of personal identity.

From the moment we receive our first ring, often a simple band from a loved one, it becomes intertwined with our sense of self. It may be a childhood gift, a memento of a significant event, or a symbol of a cherished relationship. This early association creates an emotional bond, imbuing the ring with personal meaning and significance.

As we grow older, rings continue to play a significant role in our lives. An engagement ring symbolizes a promise of eternal love and commitment, marking a pivotal moment in a romantic relationship. A wedding ring, exchanged during a sacred ceremony, signifies the union of two souls and the lifelong bond they share. These rings become tangible representations of love, hope, and the enduring power of human connection.

Beyond their sentimental value, rings can also be powerful tools for self-expression. The choice of metal, gemstone, and design reflects personal style and preferences. A minimalist silver band might appeal to those who value simplicity and understated elegance, while a bold statement ring with a vibrant gemstone might express a more flamboyant and expressive personality.

Furthermore, rings can be used to signify membership in a particular group or affiliation. Class rings, fraternity rings, and military rings serve as symbols of belonging and shared experiences, fostering a sense of community and camaraderie.

In conclusion, the ring, seemingly a small and insignificant object, holds a profound connection to the self. It serves as a symbol of love, commitment, and personal identity, reflecting our hopes, dreams, and the milestones that shape our lives. From the first childhood ring to the cherished wedding band, these pieces of jewelry become intertwined with our sense of self, creating a lasting legacy that transcends time.

Chapter 22

The Flavor of Life: Sweet and Sour

The interplay of sweet and sour flavors extends beyond the culinary realm, mirroring the complexities of the human experience. Just as these contrasting tastes dance on the palate, our lives are a constant interplay of joy and sorrow, triumph and defeat, light and shadow.

The sweetness in life represents the joys and pleasures we encounter – love, success, moments of pure bliss. It's the comforting embrace of family, the thrill of a new adventure, the satisfaction of a hard-earned victory. These sweet moments nourish our souls, providing us with energy and a sense of fulfillment.

However, life is not always a bed of roses. We inevitably encounter challenges and setbacks, experiences that can leave a sour taste in our mouths. These experiences, such as loss, disappointment, and adversity, can be painful and difficult to navigate. Yet, they also serve a crucial purpose. They teach us valuable lessons, build resilience, and deepen our understanding of ourselves and the world around us.

The beauty of the human experience lies in our ability to navigate these contrasting experiences with grace and resilience. Just as a well-balanced sweet and sour dish offers a symphony of flavors, our lives become richer when we embrace both the joys and sorrows, the triumphs and setbacks.

Learning to appreciate the sour moments, to learn from them and grow stronger, allows us to savor the sweetness of life even more deeply. It's about finding balance, recognizing that the shadows make the light shine brighter, and that the sour notes add depth and complexity to the overall melody of our lives.

In essence, the sweet and sour flavors of life mirror the complexities of our own human experience. By embracing both the joys and sorrows, we can cultivate a deeper understanding of ourselves and live a more fulfilling and meaningful life.

Chapter 23

The Bucket Within

The meek bucket, often overlooked as a simple household item, holds a surprisingly profound connection to the self. Beyond its utilitarian function, it can be a powerful symbol, a tool for self-discovery, and a reminder of our interconnectedness.

For many, the bucket evokes childhood memories. It's the vessel used for sandcastle building on the beach, for catching fireflies on a summer night, and for collecting rainwater during a storm. These early experiences create an emotional bond, imbuing the bucket with a sense of nostalgia and a connection to a simpler, more carefree time.

Beyond its nostalgic value, the bucket can be a powerful symbol of our capacity for both creation and destruction. It can be used to build, to nurture, and to bring forth new life, as in the case of a gardener planting seeds. Conversely, it can also be used to discard, to let go of the old and make space for the new. This duality mirrors the ebb and flow of life, the constant cycle of creation and destruction that shapes our existence.

Furthermore, the bucket can be a tool for self-discovery. The act of filling a bucket with water, carrying it carefully, and then emptying it can be a meditative practice, a reminder of the impermanence of all things. It can also be a metaphor for our own emotional and spiritual journeys, the constant process of filling ourselves with love, joy, and inspiration, and then sharing those gifts with the world.

Finally, the bucket can be a reminder of our interconnectedness. Whether it's sharing water with a thirsty animal, collecting rainwater for a community garden, or simply using it to wash our hands, the bucket connects us to the natural world and to the needs of others. It reminds us that we are all interconnected, and that our actions have an impact on the world around us.

In conclusion, the bucket, seemingly a simple and insignificant object, holds a profound connection to the self. It is a symbol of childhood memories, a reflection of our capacity for creation and destruction, a tool for self-discovery, and a reminder of our interconnectedness. By observing the humble bucket, we can gain valuable insights into our own lives and our place in the world.

Chapter 24

Specs: A Window to the Soul

The pair of eyeglasses, is often seen as a mere corrective device, holds a surprisingly profound connection to the self. Beyond their functional purpose, they can be a powerful symbol, a reflection of personal style, and even a tool for self-discovery.

For many, the need for eyeglasses marks a significant transition, recognition of changing eyesight and the passage of time. This can be a bittersweet moment, a reminder of the fleeting nature of youth and the inevitability of aging. However, it can also be an opportunity for self-acceptance and a chance to embrace a new phase of life.

The choice of eyeglasses has become a significant aspect of personal style. From classic frames to bold, avant-garde designs, eyeglasses have evolved into a fashion statement, allowing individuals to express their unique personalities and individuality. The careful selection of frames, considering factors such as face shape, skin tone, and personal style, can be a form of self-expression, a way to project a desired image to the world.

Furthermore, eyeglasses can serve as a tool for self-discovery. They can enhance our perception of the world, bringing into sharper focus the details we might otherwise miss. This heightened awareness can lead to new insights and a deeper appreciation for the beauty and complexity of the world around us.

For some, eyeglasses can also be a source of confidence. They can help to correct vision problems, improving self-esteem and allowing individuals to participate more fully in social and professional activities.

In conclusion, the pair of eyeglasses, seemingly a simple and utilitarian object, holds a surprising depth of meaning. They are more than just corrective lenses; they are a reflection of our changing selves, a tool for self-expression, and a window to the world. By embracing the need for eyeglasses, we can embrace a new phase of life, enhance our perception of the world, and discover new facets of our own identities.

Chapter 25

Self-Care and Self-Expression

The meek comb, often taken for granted as a simple grooming tool, holds a surprisingly profound connection to the self. Beyond its functional purpose, it can be a symbol of self-care, a reflection of personal style, and even a tool for self-discovery.

For many, the act of combing their hair is a deeply personal and intimate ritual. It's a moment of quiet reflection, a time to connect with oneself and to attend to the details of one's appearance. This daily act of self-care can be a source of comfort and grounding, a way to start the day with a sense of calm and intention.

The choice of comb can also be a reflection of personal style and values. A wooden comb might appeal to those who appreciate natural materials and sustainable practices, while a sleek, minimalist design might resonate with those who value simplicity and functionality. The intricate carvings on a traditional comb can reflect cultural heritage and personal beliefs, connecting the individual to their roots and traditions.

Furthermore, the act of combing one's hair can be a form of self-expression. The style of the hair itself, whether it's a carefully constructed updo or a carefree cascade of curls, is often a reflection of one's personality and mood. The comb, as the tool that shapes and defines this style, becomes an extension of that self-expression.

Beyond its practical and aesthetic functions, the comb can also be a metaphor for the process of self-discovery. Just as the comb untangles and smooths the hair, we can use introspection and self-reflection to untangle the complexities of our own minds, to smooth out the rough edges of our personalities, and to cultivate inner peace and harmony.

In conclusion, the humble comb, seemingly a simple and insignificant object, holds a surprising depth of meaning. It is a symbol of self-care, a reflection of personal style, and a tool for self-discovery. By paying attention to the act of combing our hair, we can gain valuable insights into our own selves and cultivate a deeper sense of self-awareness and well-being.

Chapter 26

Exploring the Connection Between Hue and Identity

Color, often perceived as a purely aesthetic phenomenon, holds a profound connection to the self. It's more than just a visual sensation; it's a powerful tool for self-expression, a reflection of our inner world, and a source of emotional resonance.

Our preferences for certain colors can be deeply personal and often reveal aspects of our personality. For example, a preference for vibrant hues like red and orange might suggest an outgoing and energetic personality, while a fondness for calming blues and greens could indicate a more introspective and peaceful nature. These color preferences often remain consistent throughout our lives, reflecting our enduring personality traits and values.

Color can also be a powerful tool for self-expression. The clothes we wear, the art we create, and the environments we choose to inhabit are all influenced by our color preferences. These choices allow us to project a desired image to the world, to communicate our mood, and to express our individuality.

Furthermore, color can have a profound impact on our emotional state. Studies have shown that certain colors can evoke specific emotions. For example, red is often associated with passion and excitement, while blue is linked to feelings of calm and tranquility. By consciously incorporating these colors into our surroundings, we can influence our mood and create an environment that supports our emotional well-being.

The use of color in therapy, known as chromotherapy, demonstrates the powerful impact of color on the mind and body. Different colors are believed to have specific healing properties, and exposure to these colors can be used to alleviate stress, improve mood, and promote overall well-being.

In conclusion, color is more than just a visual sensation; it's a deeply personal and multifaceted aspect of the human experience. It's a reflection of our inner world, a tool for self-expression, and a source of emotional resonance. By understanding the impact of color on our lives, we can harness its power to create a more fulfilling and meaningful existence.

Chapter 27

The Self in the Frame

The photograph, a seemingly simple image captured in a moment, holds a profound connection to the self. It's more than just a visual record; it's a window into the past, a reflection of our memories, and a powerful tool for self-discovery.

Photographs serve as tangible reminders of our lives. They capture fleeting moments, preserving precious memories that might otherwise fade with time. A family portrait evokes feelings of love and belonging, while a snapshot from a childhood vacation transports us back to a time of carefree joy. These images become cherished possessions, connecting us to our past and providing a sense of continuity and belonging.

Furthermore, photographs can be powerful tools for self-reflection. Looking back at old photos can trigger a cascade of memories, prompting us to reflect on our growth, our experiences, and the people who have shaped our lives. We can see how we've changed physically, emotionally, and spiritually, and gain a deeper understanding of our journey.

Photographs also play a crucial role in shaping our self-perception. The images we see of ourselves in the mirror, in social media, and in family albums contribute to our sense of self-worth and identity. The way we are portrayed in these images can influence how we see ourselves and how we present ourselves to the world.

In the age of social media, the role of photography in shaping our self-perception has become even more pronounced. The curated images we share online often present an idealized version of ourselves, leading to feelings of inadequacy and social comparison. It's important to remember that these images often represent a carefully constructed and filtered reality, and that true self-worth comes from within.

In conclusion, the photograph, seemingly a simple image captured in a moment, holds a profound connection to the self. It's a window into the past, a reflection of our memories, and a powerful tool for self-discovery. By consciously engaging with the photographs in our lives, we can gain a deeper understanding of ourselves and our place in the world.

Chapter 28

Attraction, Repulsion, and the Human Experience

The humble magnet, often associated with simple children's toys and refrigerator decorations, holds a surprisingly profound connection to the self. Beyond its ability to attract metal, it can be a metaphor for the forces that shape our lives, a reflection of our own inner desires, and a reminder of the interconnectedness of all things.

Just as magnets are drawn to certain metals and repelled by others, we are drawn to certain people, experiences, and ideas while simultaneously being repelled by others. These attractions and repulsions are often subconscious, driven by our values, beliefs, and subconscious desires. Understanding these inherent forces can provide valuable insights into our own motivations and the relationships we form with others.

The concept of "like attracts like" is often associated with magnets, and this principle can also be applied to our own lives. Our thoughts, beliefs, and actions create an energetic field that attracts similar energies into our lives. By cultivating positive thoughts and engaging in positive actions, we can attract more positive experiences into our lives. Conversely, negative thoughts and actions can create a self-fulfilling prophecy, attracting more negativity into our lives.

Furthermore, magnets serve as a reminder of the interconnectedness of all things. Just as the magnetic field extends beyond the physical boundaries of the magnet itself, our actions and choices have a ripple effect, influencing not only ourselves but also those around us. Recognizing this interconnectedness can inspire us to act with compassion and consideration, understanding that our choices have consequences that extend beyond ourselves.

In conclusion, the seemingly simple magnet offers a powerful metaphor for the forces that shape our lives. By understanding the principles of attraction and repulsion, and recognizing the interconnectedness of all things, we can gain valuable insights into our own motivations, cultivate positive relationships, and create a more fulfilling and meaningful life.

Chapter 29

The Art of Display

The wall hanger is often dismissed as a mere utilitarian object, holds a surprisingly profound connection to the self. Beyond its functional purpose of holding items, it can be a reflection of personal style, a symbol of accomplishment, and a reminder of our interconnectedness.

The choice of wall hanger can be a subtle yet significant expression of personal taste. A rustic wooden hanger might appeal to those who value natural materials and a connection to nature. A sleek, minimalist design might resonate with those who appreciate clean lines and modern aesthetics. The decorative details, such as intricate carvings or colorful embellishments, can reflect individual preferences and add a touch of personality to any space.

Furthermore, wall hangers can serve as symbols of accomplishment and personal growth. A framed certificate, a prized medal, or a cherished piece of artwork displayed on a wall hanger can be a source of pride and motivation. These objects represent our achievements, our passions, and the milestones we have reached throughout our lives.

Wall hangers also play a role in shaping the ambiance of our living spaces. The objects we choose to display on our walls – photographs, artwork, and travel souvenirs – tell a story about ourselves, our experiences, and our values. These curated collections reflect our interests, our memories, and the things that bring us joy.

In conclusion, the wall hanger, seemingly a simple and insignificant object, holds a surprising depth of meaning. It's more than just a hook; it's a reflection of our personal style, a symbol of our accomplishments, and a window into our inner world. By consciously selecting and displaying objects on our walls, we can create spaces that are not only aesthetically pleasing but also deeply personal and meaningful.

Chapter 30

Unlocking the Self: Access and Responsibility

The deferential key, often taken for granted as a simple tool for access, holds a surprisingly profound connection to the self. Beyond its functional purpose, it can be a symbol of freedom, responsibility, and personal identity.

For many, the possession of keys signifies a sense of independence and autonomy. The ability to unlock one's own home, car, or office provides a feeling of control and ownership. It's a tangible symbol of personal freedom and the ability to come and go as one pleases.

Keys can also be powerful symbols of responsibility. The keys to a home represent the responsibility of maintaining a safe and comfortable living space. The keys to a car signify the responsibility of driving safely and responsibly. These keys, while granting access, also carry with them a sense of duty and obligation.

Furthermore, keys can hold significant sentimental value. The keys to a childhood home can evoke nostalgic memories and a sense of longing for the past. A set of keys received as a gift from a loved one can symbolize trust, affection, and a shared sense of belonging. These keys become more than just tools for access; they become cherished keepsakes, imbued with personal meaning and emotional resonance.

In the digital age, with the rise of keyless entry systems, the symbolic significance of keys may seem diminished. However, the underlying principles remain the same. Access, responsibility, and the sense of ownership that keys represent continue to hold profound meaning in our lives.

In conclusion, the seemingly simple key holds a surprising depth of meaning. It's a symbol of freedom and responsibility, a reminder of our personal journeys, and a connection to our past, present, and future. By reflecting on the significance of the keys in our lives, we can gain a deeper understanding of our own sense of autonomy, our responsibilities, and our place in the world.

Chapter 31.

Finding Shelter: Exploring the Relationship between Self and Support

The umbrella, a seemingly simple object, offers a profound metaphor for the human experience. It provides shelter from the elements, a temporary refuge from the storm of life. But its effectiveness depends entirely on how it is used, reflecting the delicate balance between self-reliance and the acceptance of external support.

When rain descends, we instinctively reach for our umbrellas. They offer a tangible shield, protecting us from the downpour. This act symbolizes our natural inclination towards self-preservation, our inherent desire to shield ourselves from harm. We strive to build our own shelters, whether it's through education, career, or relationships, seeking security and stability in a world that can often feel chaotic.

However, the umbrella's effectiveness is limited. In a torrential downpour, even the strongest umbrella may fail to keep us completely dry. We might get soaked despite our best efforts. This highlights the limitations of individual effort and the recognition of forces beyond our control. Life throws curveballs, challenges that no amount of personal resilience can fully mitigate.

This realization can be humbling, even frightening. It can lead to feelings of helplessness and a sense of being adrift in a sea of uncertainty. But it can also be a powerful catalyst for growth. When we acknowledge our limitations, we become more open to seeking and accepting help.

Just as we might seek shelter under a larger awning or share an umbrella with a companion, we learn to rely on others for support. We discover the strength in community, the power of human connection. We learn to lean on friends, family, and mentors, recognizing that our journey is not solely our own.

Furthermore, the umbrella itself can be a symbol of personal expression. Its color, pattern, and size can reflect our unique personality and style. It becomes an extension of ourselves, a way to showcase our individuality in the midst of a shared experience.

However, excessive reliance on the umbrella can also be detrimental. If we become so dependent on external support that we fail to develop our own inner strength and resilience, we become vulnerable. We must learn to navigate life's challenges with a balance of self-reliance and the acceptance of help. We must cultivate our own inner umbrella, a sense of self-worth and inner strength that can weather any storm.

Ultimately, the umbrella serves as a reminder of the delicate dance between self-reliance and interdependence. It encourages us to embrace our individuality while recognizing the importance of community. It teaches us to navigate life's challenges with a combination of resilience, resourcefulness, and the grace to accept a helping hand when needed.

Just as the umbrella provides shelter from the rain, allowing us to continue our journey, so too must we cultivate a sense of self that provides us with the strength and resilience to navigate the storms of life. We must learn to open ourselves to the support of others while nurturing our own inner strength, creating a balance that allows us to flourish in the face of adversity.

Chapter 32.

Boundaries, Connection, and the Journey Within

The envelope, a seemingly mundane object, offers a surprising depth of metaphor when considered in relation to the self. Its function – to contain and protect – mirrors the human need for both boundaries and vulnerability.

At its core, the envelope represents the self as a container. It holds within it our thoughts, feelings, experiences, and deepest desires. This container provides a sense of identity, a defined space where our individuality resides. Just as an envelope safeguards its contents from the outside world, the self acts as a protective barrier, shielding our inner world from the potential chaos and intrusions of external forces.

This protective function, however, can sometimes become a barrier to growth and connection. Just as an unopened envelope remains a mystery, an overly rigid self can hinder genuine intimacy and understanding. It can create a sense of isolation, preventing us from sharing our true selves with others and from fully experiencing the richness of human connection.

The act of opening an envelope signifies a willingness to engage with the unknown. It represents a vulnerability, a trust in the receiver to handle the contents with care. Similarly, opening ourselves to others requires a degree of courage and vulnerability. It involves sharing our thoughts, feelings, and experiences, even when there is a risk of rejection or misunderstanding.

The process of sealing an envelope also carries symbolic weight. It represents the act of intention, of consciously choosing what to share and what to keep private. This reflects the careful curation of our self-presentation, the way we choose to reveal ourselves to the world. We decide which aspects of ourselves to emphasize, which to conceal, and how to present ourselves to others.

The envelope's journey, from sender to receiver, mirrors the human experience of connection. It represents the act of communication, the transmission of thoughts and emotions across space and time. This journey can be fraught with uncertainties. Will the envelope reach its destination? Will it be received with the intended meaning? These uncertainties reflect the inherent risks and vulnerabilities involved in human interaction.

Furthermore, the envelope can be seen as a symbol of potential. It carries within it the possibility of transformation, the seeds of new ideas and experiences. Just as a letter within an envelope can contain words of love, hope, or inspiration, the self holds the potential for growth, creativity, and profound connection.

In conclusion, the envelope, though seemingly simple, offers a rich tapestry of metaphors for the human experience. It reflects the interplay between self-protection and vulnerability, the importance of both boundaries and connection. By understanding the symbolic significance of the envelope, we can gain deeper insights into the nature of the self, the complexities of human interaction, and the ongoing journey of self-discovery.

Chapter 33.

The Power of Voice and the Journey of Self-Discovery

The relationship between self and speaker offers a fascinating lens through which to examine human communication and identity. Just as a speaker transforms electrical signals into audible sound waves, the self acts as a transducer, converting inner thoughts and emotions into external expressions.

At its core, the speaker is a tool for amplification. It allows a voice, perhaps initially faint or inaudible, to reach a wider audience. Similarly, the self, through communication, amplifies its inner world. Thoughts, feelings, and ideas that may have remained confined to the realm of the internal become externalized, shared, and potentially amplified within the social sphere.

However, the relationship between self and speaker is not merely one of simple amplification. The act of speaking inevitably shapes the self. In the process of articulating our thoughts, we refine them, clarify them, and often discover new layers of meaning and understanding. The very act of giving voice to our inner world can lead to new insights and perspectives.

Furthermore, the speaker, with its various settings and controls, allows for a degree of manipulation and nuance in the delivery of sound. Similarly, the self possesses a degree of agency in how it chooses to express itself. We can modulate our tone, adjust our volume, and select our words carefully to convey specific messages and evoke particular responses.

The speaker, however, is not merely a passive instrument. It requires input, a source of energy to produce sound. Similarly, the self requires inner resources, such as emotional intelligence and self-awareness, to effectively communicate. Without these internal resources, our expressions may lack clarity, authenticity, or impact.

The speaker, with its potential for both amplification and distortion, serves as a powerful metaphor for the complexities of human communication. It highlights the delicate balance between self-expression and self-preservation, the power of voice and the responsibility that comes with it. By understanding the intricate relationship between self and speaker, we can gain deeper insights into the nature of communication, the construction of identity, and the profound impact that our words can have on the world around us.

Chapter 34.

The Boat and the Human Experience

The boat, a vessel designed to navigate the waters, offers a rich and multifaceted metaphor for the human experience. Just as a boat navigates through currents and tides, so too does the self traverse the ever-changing sea of life, encountering challenges, embracing opportunities, and striving for its destination.

The very act of constructing a boat requires careful planning and craftsmanship. It demands a deep understanding of the materials, the environment, and the intended purpose of the vessel. Similarly, the development of the self requires conscious effort, careful cultivation of skills, and a clear understanding of one's values and aspirations.

The boat's journey is inherently uncertain. It faces the unpredictable whims of the weather, the dangers of hidden rocks, and the ever-present threat of storms. Likewise, the path of life is rarely straightforward. We encounter unexpected obstacles, experience unforeseen setbacks, and must constantly adapt to changing circumstances.

The boat's success often depends on its ability to navigate effectively. It must possess the necessary tools and techniques to steer a course, to adjust its sails to the wind, and to weather the storms. Similarly, the self requires a repertoire of skills – resilience, adaptability, problem-solving abilities – to navigate the complexities of life.

The boat, however, is not merely a passive vessel. It requires a skilled captain, someone with the knowledge and experience to guide it safely through treacherous waters. Similarly, the self requires conscious direction, a sense of purpose, and the inner strength to steer its own course.

The boat, at its core, is a means of transportation, a tool for reaching a desired destination. Whether it's a journey across a vast ocean or a simple voyage down a tranquil river, the boat facilitates movement and progress. Similarly, the self, through its actions and choices, propels itself towards its goals, striving for personal growth and fulfillment.

Furthermore, the boat can be a symbol of community. It can represent the shared experience of a crew working together towards a common goal, the interdependence that is essential for successful navigation. Similarly, the self thrives within a supportive community, drawing strength and inspiration from the connections it fosters with others.

In conclusion, the boat, with its inherent symbolism of journey, navigation, and community, offers a profound metaphor for the human experience. It reminds us of the importance of self-awareness, resilience, and the pursuit of our goals. It encourages us to navigate the complexities of life with courage, grace, and a sense of shared purpose, always striving towards a brighter horizon.

Chapter 35

Adornment and Entanglement

The anklet, a simple adornment often overlooked, offers a surprisingly rich metaphor for the human experience. It is a symbol of both constraint and liberation, a reminder of both individuality and interconnectedness.

Worn around the ankle, the anklet represents the delicate balance between freedom and restriction. It adorns and embellishes, but also subtly confines. This duality mirrors the human condition, where we constantly navigate the tension between our desire for autonomy and the inherent limitations imposed by societal norms, relationships, and our own inner struggles.

The anklet, often made of precious metals or adorned with intricate designs, can be seen as a symbol of self-expression. It is a way to adorn oneself, to showcase individuality and personal style. Just as an anklet reflects the wearer's unique taste and personality, so too does the self express itself through its choices, its actions, and its interactions with the world.

The sound of an anklet jingling as it moves can be both captivating and mesmerizing. This sound symbolizes the rhythm of life, the constant ebb and flow of experiences, thoughts, and emotions. It represents the dynamic nature of the self, the ever-changing interplay of internal and external forces.

The anklet, often passed down through generations, can also be a symbol of heritage and connection. It represents the link to ancestors, the shared history and cultural traditions that shape our identity. This connection to the past provides a sense of grounding, a reminder of our roots and the lineage from which we have emerged.

However, the anklet can also represent a burden, a symbol of societal expectations or the weight of past experiences. It can feel like a constraint, limiting freedom of movement and expression. This reflects the ways in which societal norms, cultural expectations, and past traumas can sometimes hinder personal growth and self-actualization.

The act of removing an anklet can be seen as an act of liberation, a shedding of constraints and a reclaiming of autonomy. It represents a breaking free from limitations, a step towards self-discovery and self-acceptance.

In conclusion, the anklet, though seemingly simple, offers a profound metaphor for the human experience. It reflects the delicate balance between freedom and constraint, the interplay of individuality and interconnectedness, and the ongoing journey of self-discovery and self-expression. By exploring the symbolism of the anklet, we can gain deeper insights into the complexities of the human condition and the ongoing quest for authenticity and freedom.

Chapter 36

A Journey of Unwrapping

The act of gift wrapping, often seen as a mere formality, offers a surprisingly rich metaphor for the human experience. It reflects the delicate balance between concealing and revealing, between the desire for protection and the need for expression.

At its core, gift wrap serves a dual purpose: to conceal the gift and to enhance its presentation. This duality mirrors the human experience, where we simultaneously strive to protect our inner selves while also seeking to express our unique identities to the world. We build emotional barriers, shielding our vulnerabilities, while also yearning for genuine connection and the opportunity to share our true selves.

The act of choosing the right wrapping paper is a form of self-expression. Patterns, colors, and textures all contribute to the overall aesthetic, reflecting the giver's personality and intentions. This resonates with the way we present ourselves to the world, the choices we make in our appearance and behavior to convey a specific image or message.

The process of carefully wrapping a gift requires attention to detail, a focus on creating something beautiful and meaningful. This parallels the effort we invest in cultivating our inner selves, in nurturing our talents, and in developing the skills and qualities that make us unique.

The act of unwrapping a gift is a moment of anticipation and excitement. It represents the unveiling of something special, the revelation of a hidden treasure. Similarly, the process of self-discovery involves peeling back the layers of our own personalities, uncovering our strengths, weaknesses, and deepest desires.

However, the act of unwrapping can also be a source of anxiety. Will the gift be as expected? Will it be appreciated? This reflects the inherent vulnerability in self-expression, the fear of rejection or judgment.

The discarded wrapping paper, often overlooked, can symbolize the transitory nature of external appearances. It reminds us that true value lies beneath the surface, in the essence of the gift itself, in the thoughtfulness and intention behind the gesture. Similarly, our external personas, while important, should not overshadow our inner selves, our true essence, our unique blend of strengths, weaknesses, and aspirations.

In conclusion, the seemingly simple act of gift wrapping offers a profound reflection on the human experience. It mirrors the delicate balance between concealment and revelation, the interplay between self-expression and self-protection, and the ongoing journey of self-discovery and self-acceptance. By understanding the deeper symbolism of gift wrapping, we can gain valuable insights into the complexities of human interaction and the importance of cultivating both our inner and outer selves.

Chapter 37

A Reflection on Joy, Burden, and Interconnectedness

The garland, a seemingly simple adornment, offers a profound metaphor for the human experience. It is a symbol of both celebration and constraint, of both beauty and burden, reflecting the complex interplay of joy, responsibility, and the delicate balance between freedom and obligation.

At its core, the garland is a collection of individual elements – flowers, leaves, beads – woven together to create a unified whole. This mirrors the human experience, where individuals, with their unique personalities and experiences, come together to form communities and societies.

The act of creating a garland requires careful selection and arrangement. It demands a sense of aesthetics, a consideration of color, texture, and overall harmony. This parallels the human endeavor to cultivate meaningful relationships, to build a harmonious and fulfilling life by carefully choosing the people and experiences that enrich our lives.

The garland, often used to adorn and celebrate, symbolizes joy, festivity, and accomplishment. It is a visual expression of happiness, a way to mark special occasions and to honor achievements. This resonates with the human desire for recognition, for our accomplishments to be acknowledged and celebrated.

However, the garland, while beautiful, can also be a source of weight and constraint. Its weight can pull down the object it adorns; its length can restrict movement. This reflects the burdens we carry, the responsibilities and expectations that can sometimes feel overwhelming.

The garland, with its interconnected elements, can also symbolize the interconnectedness of all beings. It reminds us that we are all part of a larger whole, that our actions and choices have an impact on others. This interconnectedness can be both a source of strength and a source of responsibility.

The act of removing a garland can be seen as a form of release, a shedding of burdens and a return to a simpler state. It can symbolize the letting go of past experiences, of overcoming obstacles, and moving forward with renewed lightness and freedom.

In conclusion, the garland, with its intricate symbolism, offers a profound reflection on the human experience. It mirrors the delicate balance between joy and responsibility, the interconnectedness of individuals within a larger whole, and the ongoing journey of growth and transformation. By exploring the deeper meaning of the garland, we can gain valuable insights into the complexities of human relationships, the importance of community, and the ongoing quest for a life that is both meaningful and fulfilling.

Chapter 38

The Turning Blades: A Reflection on Emotional Equilibrium

The fan, a seemingly simple device designed to circulate air, offers a surprisingly rich metaphor for the human experience. It reflects the constant interplay between internal and external forces, the need for both cooling and stimulation, and the delicate balance between comfort and control.

At its core, the fan is a tool for regulating temperature. It provides relief from the heat, creating a sense of comfort and refreshment. This mirrors the human need for emotional regulation, the constant effort to maintain inner balance in the face of external pressures and internal turmoil.

The fan's operation depends on external forces – electricity, wind, or manual effort. Similarly, human well-being is influenced by external factors – relationships, environment, and social circumstances. We are constantly adapting to our surroundings, seeking to create a comfortable and supportive environment for ourselves.

The fan, with its adjustable speed and direction, allows for a degree of control over the airflow. This reflects the human desire for agency, the need to exert some control over our circumstances. We strive to shape our lives, to make choices that create a sense of order and predictability in an often chaotic world.

However, excessive reliance on the fan can be detrimental. Constant exposure to artificial cooling can weaken our natural resilience to heat. Similarly, excessive attempts to control our environment can lead to a sense of rigidity, hindering our ability to adapt and grow.

The fan, with its rotating blades, can also represent the cyclical nature of life, the constant ebb and flow of emotions, the ever-changing interplay of internal and external forces. It reminds us that life is not static, that change is inevitable, and that we must learn to adapt and find comfort within the flow of life.

The fan, in its simplest form, is a tool for comfort and refreshment. But it can also be a source of inspiration, a reminder of the importance of finding balance, cultivating inner resilience, and embracing the ever-changing currents of life.

In conclusion, the fan, with its seemingly simple function, offers a profound metaphor for the human experience. It reflects the interplay between internal and external forces, the need for both comfort and stimulation, and the ongoing quest for balance and well-being. By exploring the deeper symbolism of the fan, we can gain valuable insights into the complexities of the human condition and the ongoing journey of self-discovery and self-actualization.

Chapter 39

Reading the World: Reading the Self

The newspaper, a seemingly mundane object, offers a surprisingly rich metaphor for the human experience. It serves as a window to the world, reflecting the complexities of society, the ebb and flow of events, and the constant evolution of our understanding.

Just as a newspaper presents a curated selection of events, the self presents a curated version of itself to the world. We choose what to share, what to conceal, and how to present ourselves to others. This act of self-presentation involves a careful selection of information, a conscious effort to shape our public image.

The newspaper, with its headlines and bold print, often emphasizes the dramatic and the sensational. This can create a distorted view of reality, focusing on the negative and sensational while downplaying the mundane and the positive. Similarly, our perceptions of ourselves and the world around us can be influenced by biases, prejudices, and the constant bombardment of information.

The newspaper, with its daily arrival, provides a sense of routine and connection to the larger world. It offers a shared experience, a common ground for discussion and debate. Similarly, our interactions with others, our engagement with society, contribute to our sense of belonging and our understanding of our place in the world.

However, excessive consumption of news can have a negative impact. Constant exposure to negativity and sensationalism can lead to anxiety, fear, and a sense of helplessness. Similarly, an overemphasis on external validation and social media can distort our self-perception and lead to feelings of inadequacy and comparison.

The newspaper, with its evolving format and content, reflects the changing nature of information dissemination. From print to digital, the medium continues to adapt to the evolving needs and preferences of its audience. Similarly, the self is constantly evolving, adapting to new experiences, new relationships, and the ever-changing demands of life.

In conclusion, the newspaper, with its multifaceted symbolism, offers a profound reflection on the human experience. It mirrors the complexities of self-presentation, the influence of external forces on our perceptions, and the ongoing journey of self-discovery and self-actualization in a world of ever-changing information. By understanding the deeper meaning of the newspaper, we can gain valuable insights into the nature of reality, the importance of critical thinking, and the ongoing quest for authenticity and meaning in our lives.

Chapter 40.

Finding Balance: The Self and the Metaphor of Containment

The humble tray, often overlooked in its simplicity, offers a surprisingly rich metaphor for the human experience. It is a vessel, a container, a platform for presentation – all of which resonate deeply with the human condition.

At its core, the tray serves as a platform, a surface upon which objects are placed and presented. This reflects the human need for a foundation, a stable base upon which to build our lives. It symbolizes the importance of establishing a sense of groundedness, a stable platform from which to navigate the complexities of life.

The tray, by its very nature, is designed to hold and support. It provides a secure and organized space for objects, preventing them from spilling or scattering. This mirrors the human need for order and structure, for a sense of control and predictability in an often chaotic world. We strive to create order in our lives, to establish routines and structures that provide a sense of stability and security.

The tray, however, is not merely a passive container. It facilitates the movement and presentation of objects. It allows us to transport items with ease, to arrange them aesthetically, and to share them with others. This reflects the human desire for connection, for sharing our experiences, our creations, and our lives with others.

The tray, with its edges and boundaries, defines a specific space. It represents the need for boundaries, for a sense of personal space and individuality. These boundaries help to define who we are, to differentiate ourselves from others, and to create a sense of personal identity.

However, the tray, with its limited capacity, can also represent the limitations of our resources and the need for careful consideration. It reminds us that our resources are finite, that we must make choices about what to prioritize and what to let go of.

The tray, in its simplicity, offers a profound reflection on the human experience. It mirrors our need for stability, order, and connection, while also acknowledging the limitations and constraints that shape our lives. By understanding the deeper symbolism of the tray, we can gain valuable insights into the complexities of the human condition, the importance of establishing a strong foundation, and the ongoing journey of navigating life with grace and intention.

Chapter 41

Ode to the Humble Hydration Hero

The humble water bottle. An innocuous object, often overlooked in the whirlwind of our daily lives. Yet, within its simple form lies a profound metaphor for self-care, discipline, and the delicate balance between our inner and outer worlds.

Think about it. A water bottle is essentially an external reminder of an internal need. It's a constant companion, a silent guardian urging us to replenish, to nourish the very essence of our being. Just as we need to hydrate our physical bodies, we need to nurture our minds and souls.

Every time we reach for our water bottle, it's a small act of self-care. It's acknowledging the importance of listening to our body's signals, of prioritizing our well-being. It's a conscious choice to break away from the distractions of the world and attend to our fundamental needs.

Furthermore, a water bottle can be a powerful symbol of discipline. Carrying it with us throughout the day requires a conscious effort, a commitment to our own health. It's about establishing a routine, a habit that supports our overall well-being. Just as we need to consistently refill our water bottle, we need to consistently nourish our minds and spirits with positive thoughts, meaningful experiences, and healthy habits.

The water bottle also mirrors the delicate balance between our inner and outer worlds. It's a tangible object that represents an intangible need. It's a bridge between our physical selves and our emotional and spiritual selves. Just as water sustains life, our inner resources – our resilience, our creativity, our compassion – sustain our well-being.

The water bottle can be a powerful tool for self-reflection. When we notice ourselves neglecting to drink, it can be a signal that we're neglecting our own needs in other areas of our lives. Perhaps we're not prioritizing rest, not allowing ourselves time for creativity, or not nurturing our relationships.

The color of our water bottle, its design, even the way we carry it, can reflect our personality. Some may prefer sleek and minimalist designs, while others gravitate towards vibrant colors and playful patterns. Some may meticulously track their water intake, while others simply enjoy the refreshing sensation of a cold drink.

Ultimately, the water bottle becomes more than just an object; it becomes an extension of ourselves. It's a symbol of our commitment to self-care, a reflection of our values, and a reminder of the importance of nurturing our inner and outer worlds.

So, the next time you reach for your water bottle, take a moment to appreciate its significance. Acknowledge the small act of self-care, the commitment to your well-being, and the delicate balance it represents. Let it be a gentle reminder to nourish yourself, to listen to your body's signals, and to cultivate a life that is both fulfilling and sustainable.

In conclusion, the water bottle, in its simplicity, offers a profound reflection on the human experience. It's a tangible reminder of our interconnectedness, our need for nourishment, and the importance of cultivating a life that is both mindful and meaningful. By paying attention to this seemingly insignificant object, we can gain valuable insights into ourselves and our relationship with the world around us.

Chapter 42

Finding Meaning in Motion: Reflections on the Bus Ride

The bus. A ubiquitous vehicle, a symbol of both mundane transit and grand adventure. For many, it's simply a means to an end, a metal box transporting them from point A to point B. But for others, the bus offers a unique window into the human experience, a microcosm of society itself.

Riding the bus can be a humbling experience. It forces us to confront the realities of shared space, to acknowledge the presence of others, their stories, their journeys. We are thrown together, a diversity of humanity, united by our shared destination, however fleeting. There's the businessman engrossed in a phone call, the student lost in a book, the elderly woman clutching her shopping bags, the weary traveler gazing out the window. Each face tells a story, a glimpse into their lives, their hopes, their anxieties.

The bus can be a source of unexpected encounters. Conversations may strike up with fellow passengers, bonds forged in shared experiences. A missed connection, a delayed departure, an unexpected detour – these unforeseen events can disrupt our carefully laid plans, forcing us to adapt, to embrace the unexpected. These disruptions, however, can also lead to unexpected discoveries, new connections, and a deeper appreciation for the present moment.

The bus offers a unique perspective on the world. It allows us to observe the ebb and flow of city life, to witness the changing landscape as we traverse different neighborhoods. We see the bustling markets, the quiet residential streets, the towering skyscrapers, the forgotten corners of the city. We become, in a sense, silent observers, absorbing the sights, sounds, and smells of the urban landscape.

Furthermore, the bus can be a powerful tool for introspection. The rhythmic motion of the vehicle, the gentle sway, can induce a state of meditative calm. It provides an opportunity to disconnect from the distractions of daily life, to reflect on our own thoughts and feelings. The journey itself becomes a metaphor for the journey of life, with its own starts and stops, its own unexpected twists and turns.

Of course, the bus ride is not always a pleasant experience. There can be overcrowding, delays, and the occasional unpleasant encounter. But even in these moments of discomfort, there are valuable lessons to be learned. We learn about patience, about resilience, about the importance of finding moments of peace amidst chaos.

In conclusion, the bus, in its ordinary existence, offers a profound reflection on the human condition. It's a space of shared experience, a window into the diverse tapestry of humanity, and a vehicle for both physical and emotional journeys. By embracing the bus ride, we embrace the unexpected, the unpredictable, and the inherent beauty of the human experience.

Chapter 43

Finding Freedom on the Tracks

The train. A symbol of progress, a testament to human ingenuity, and for many, a constant companion on life's journey. More than just a mode of transport, the train offers a unique perspective on the self, a reflection of our inner landscapes and the ever-shifting currents of our lives.

The rhythmic chugging of the engine, the rhythmic clicking of the wheels on the tracks – these sounds create a hypnotic rhythm, a lullaby that can lull the mind into a state of introspection. As the train hurtles forward, leaving behind a trail of dust and fleeting impressions, we are afforded the opportunity to disconnect from the distractions of everyday life and delve into the depths of our own consciousness.

The train window becomes a frame, a constantly shifting canvas that reflects the ever-changing external world. Rolling hills give way to bustling cities, vast plains stretch out towards the horizon, and the sky transforms from a vibrant blue to a fiery orange as the sun dips below the horizon. These fleeting glimpses of the outside world mirror the fleeting nature of our own experiences, the constant flux of emotions, thoughts, and sensations that shape our inner lives.

The train journey can be a solitary experience, a time for contemplation and reflection. It can also be a time for unexpected encounters, for chance conversations with fellow passengers, for forging fleeting connections with strangers. The train, in essence, becomes a microcosm of society, a melting pot of cultures, backgrounds, and experiences.

The delays, the detours, the unexpected stops – these unforeseen events can disrupt our carefully laid plans, forcing us to adapt, to embrace the unexpected. These disruptions, however, can also lead to unexpected discoveries, new perspectives, and a deeper appreciation for the present moment.

The train, with its inherent limitations, can also serve as a metaphor for our own limitations. We are bound by time and space, by the constraints of our own bodies and minds. Yet, within these limitations, there is also a sense of freedom, a sense of possibility. The train, despite its predetermined route, carries us towards an unknown destination, a future filled with both promise and uncertainty.

In conclusion, the train, in its very essence, offers a profound reflection on the human condition. It's a vehicle for both physical and emotional journeys, a space for introspection and connection, a mirror that reflects the ever-changing landscapes of our inner and outer worlds. By embracing the train journey, we embrace the journey of life itself, with all its inherent beauty, its inherent challenges, and its inherent uncertainty.

Chapter 44

A Symbol of Tradition and Transformation

The pipe. A seemingly simple object, yet steeped in symbolism, history, and personal meaning. More than just a conduit for water or gas, the pipe can become an extension of oneself, a reflection of our inner world, and a source of profound contemplation.

For the craftsman, the pipe might represent hours of meticulous labor, the satisfaction of creating something with their own hands. The wood, carefully selected and shaped, becomes a testament to their skill and artistry. Each pipe, unique in its grain and form, becomes a reflection of the craftsman's individual style and personality.

For the smoker, the pipe can become a cherished companion, a source of comfort and solace. The act of smoking, slow and deliberate, can be a meditative practice, a time for reflection and introspection. The smoke, curling upwards, can symbolize thoughts and ideas, rising from the depths of the subconscious.

The pipe can also be a symbol of tradition and heritage. In many cultures, pipe smoking has been an integral part of social rituals, a means of fostering community and sharing stories. The act of passing a pipe, a gesture of trust and camaraderie, can deepen bonds and strengthen relationships.

The pipe can also be a source of contemplation. As the smoker draws on the pipe, they may ponder the nature of existence, the fleeting nature of time, the interconnectedness of all things. The smoke, swirling and dissipating, can serve as a reminder of the impermanence of all things, the constant flux of change and transformation.

However, the pipe is not without its complexities. It can be a symbol of addiction, of a dependence that can consume and control. It can be a source of controversy, a subject of debate and social stigma.

Ultimately, the meaning of the pipe is subjective, unique to each individual. It can be a symbol of artistry, of relaxation, of tradition, of contemplation, or of something entirely different. It can be a source of pleasure, of addiction, or of profound introspection.

In conclusion, the pipe, in its simplicity, offers a profound reflection on the human experience. It's an object that can be both a source of comfort and a source of contention, a symbol of both creativity and addiction. By exploring the deeper meaning of the pipe, we can gain valuable insights into ourselves, our relationships with others, and our place in the world.

Chapter 45

A Reflection on Responsibility

The tap, a seemingly mundane object, often taken for granted, yet deeply intertwined with our daily lives. More than just a conduit for water, the tap offers a unique reflection of our relationship with the natural world, our sense of responsibility, and our own inner selves.

The simple act of turning a tap can evoke a range of emotions. The rush of cold water on a hot day provides instant relief, a sense of refreshment and rejuvenation. The steady flow of warm water from the faucet can be comforting, a reminder of warmth and security.

The tap also serves as a constant reminder of our dependence on a finite resource. Water, essential for life, is not an infinite commodity. The act of turning on the tap, therefore, carries with it a sense of responsibility. We are reminded of our impact on the environment, the importance of conservation, and the need to use this precious resource wisely.

The tap can also be a source of contemplation. As the water flows, we can observe its movement, its fluidity, its ever-changing form. This can be a meditative experience, a reminder of the impermanence of all things, the constant flux of change and transformation.

Furthermore, the tap can be a symbol of our connection to the natural world. Water, the source of all life, connects us to the earth, to the oceans, to the rivers that flow through our landscapes. The act of turning on the tap, therefore, connects us to a larger ecosystem, a reminder of our place within the interconnected web of life.

The tap can also be a source of both comfort and anxiety. In times of drought or water scarcity, the tap can become a source of worry, a reminder of our vulnerability and dependence on a fragile ecosystem.

Ultimately, the tap, in its simplicity, offers a profound reflection on the human condition. It's a reminder of our dependence on the natural world, our responsibility to use resources wisely, and our interconnectedness with all living things. By paying attention to this seemingly insignificant object, we can gain valuable insights into ourselves, our relationship with the environment, and our place in the grand scheme of things.

Chapter 46

A Reflection on Connection and Isolation

The laptop, a ubiquitous device, a portal to a digital world, and for many, an extension of their very selves. More than just a tool for work or entertainment, the laptop offers a unique reflection of our inner lives, our aspirations, and our evolving relationship with technology.

The laptop screen, a luminous rectangle, can become a window to a myriad of experiences. It connects us to loved ones across continents, allows us to explore distant lands through virtual travel, and provides access to an infinite well of information. It's a platform for creativity, allowing us to express ourselves through writing, music, and art.

The laptop can also be a source of both inspiration and distraction. It can be a tool for productivity, enabling us to work efficiently and achieve our goals. However, it can also be a source of procrastination, a black hole that sucks us into a vortex of social media, online shopping, and endless scrolling.

The laptop can be a mirror to our inner world. The websites we visit, the content we consume, the people we connect with online – all these choices reflect our interests, our values, and our deepest desires. The way we interact with the laptop, whether with frustration or ease, can reveal our levels of patience, our adaptability to new technologies, and our overall comfort with the digital world.

The laptop can also be a source of both connection and isolation. It can connect us to a global community, allowing us to build relationships with people from all walks of life. However, it can also lead to feelings of isolation and loneliness, as we spend more time interacting with screens and less time with real-life human beings.

Furthermore, the laptop can be a symbol of our evolving relationship with technology. As technology continues to advance, our relationship with our laptops will continue to evolve. We are constantly adapting to new interfaces, new software, and new ways of interacting with the digital world.

In conclusion, the laptop, in its seemingly simple form, offers a profound reflection on the human condition. It's a tool that can both empower and enslave, connect and isolate, inspire and distract. By understanding our relationship with our laptops, we can gain valuable insights into ourselves, our values, and our place in the ever-evolving digital age.

Chapter 47

Finding Comfort in the Glow

The table lamp, a seemingly insignificant object, often relegated to the background of our living spaces. Yet, within its simple form lies a profound reflection of our inner selves, our relationships with light and shadow, and our need for both illumination and intimacy.

The table lamp, with its soft glow, creates a warm and inviting atmosphere. It casts a gentle light, illuminating a corner of the room, creating a cozy nook for reading, writing, or simply contemplation. This localized illumination can be a source of comfort, a refuge from the harsh glare of overhead lighting.

The table lamp, in its various forms, can be a reflection of our personal style. The sleek, minimalist design might appeal to those who value simplicity and functionality. The ornate, antique lamp might resonate with those who appreciate history and tradition. The whimsical, handcrafted lamp might reflect a playful and bohemian spirit.

The table lamp can also be a source of inspiration. The interplay of light and shadow, the way the light dances on the walls and surfaces, can spark creativity and imagination. It can be a source of comfort during long hours of work, providing a warm and inviting atmosphere that helps to ease the mind and body.

The table lamp can also be a source of intimacy. Its soft glow creates a sense of coziness and seclusion, perfect for intimate conversations, quiet moments of reflection, or simply enjoying a good book. It can be a comforting presence in the evening hours, a beacon of warmth and security in the darkness.

Furthermore, the table lamp can be a symbol of our need for both illumination and darkness. Just as we need light to navigate the world, we also need darkness for rest and rejuvenation. The table lamp, with its controlled illumination, allows us to find a balance between these two opposing forces.

In conclusion, the table lamp, in its seemingly simple form, offers a profound reflection on the human experience. It's a source of both light and shadow, a reflection of our personal style, and a symbol of our need for both illumination and intimacy. By paying attention to this seemingly insignificant object, we can gain valuable insights into ourselves, our relationship with our environment, and the delicate balance between light and darkness.

Chapter 48

A Symbol of Life's Journey

The bag, an everyday object, often taken for granted, yet deeply intertwined with our daily lives. More than just a container for our belongings, the bag offers a unique reflection of our personalities, our lifestyles, and our journeys through life.

The choice of bag can be a powerful statement. The sleek, minimalist backpack might appeal to the adventurous traveler, while the classic leather tote might resonate with the discerning professional. The oversized duffel bag might be the preferred choice for the athlete, while the whimsical tote bag might reflect a playful and bohemian spirit.

The contents of our bags also offer a glimpse into our inner selves. The meticulously organized bag, with every item having its designated place, might reflect a personality that values order and efficiency. The overflowing bag, bursting at the seams with forgotten treasures, might suggest a more carefree and spontaneous approach to life.

The bag can be a source of both comfort and anxiety. It can be a source of security, a familiar companion that provides a sense of stability and order in an ever-changing world. However, it can also be a source of anxiety, a constant reminder of the weight of our possessions, the responsibilities we carry, and the burdens we bear.

The bag can be a symbol of our journeys, both literal and metaphorical. As we travel from place to place, our bags carry our stories with them. The worn-out backpack might tell tales of far-off adventures, while the elegant handbag might whisper of glamorous soirées.

Furthermore, the bag can be a reflection of our changing needs and priorities. The backpack of the carefree student might give way to the briefcase of the ambitious professional, which in turn might be replaced by the diaper bag of the new parent.

In conclusion, the bag, in its seemingly simple form, offers a profound reflection on the human experience. It's a reflection of our personalities, our lifestyles, and our journeys through life. It's a container for our belongings, but also for our memories, our hopes, and our dreams. By paying attention to this seemingly insignificant object, we can gain valuable insights into ourselves, our relationships with the world, and the ever-evolving nature of our lives.

Chapter 49

The Folder: A Symbol of Control

The folder, a seemingly mundane object, often relegated to the background of our desks and drawers. Yet, within its simple form lies a profound reflection of our inner lives, our organizational tendencies, and our relationship with information.

The folder, with its capacity to contain and organize, reflects our need for order and structure. We strive to impose order on the chaos of information, to categorize and compartmentalize our thoughts and ideas. The act of filing, of placing documents in their designated folders, can be a therapeutic exercise, a way to bring a sense of control to the ever-expanding universe of information.

The choice of folder can be a subtle reflection of our personality. The sleek, minimalist folder might appeal to those who value efficiency and simplicity. The colorful, patterned folder might reflect a more playful and expressive personality. The worn-out, well-loved folder might hold sentimental value, a testament to past projects and accomplishments.

The contents of our folders offer a glimpse into our lives, our interests, and our aspirations. The academic folder might be filled with research papers and lecture notes, while the professional folder might contain important contracts and presentations. The personal folder might hold cherished memories, photographs, and personal letters.

The folder can also be a source of both comfort and anxiety. It can be a source of comfort, providing a sense of security and order in a chaotic world. However, it can also be a source of anxiety, a reminder of unfinished projects, missed deadlines, and the ever-growing mountain of information that we must contend with.

Furthermore, the folder can be a symbol of our evolving relationship with information. In the digital age, the traditional folder is being replaced by digital folders, cloud storage, and other forms of electronic organization. These new technologies offer new possibilities for organizing and accessing information, but they also raise new challenges and questions about privacy, security, and the long-term preservation of data.

In conclusion, the folder, in its seemingly simple form, offers a profound reflection on the human experience. It's a reflection of our need for order, our relationship with information, and our evolving relationship with technology. By paying attention to this seemingly insignificant object, we can gain valuable insights into ourselves, our work habits, and our place in the ever-evolving information age.

Chapter 50

A Reflection on Freedom and Constraint

The road, an endless ribbon of asphalt, stretching out towards the horizon, a symbol of both freedom and constraint. More than just a means of transportation, the road offers a unique reflection of our inner lives, our journeys, and our relationship with the world.

The open road can be a source of exhilaration, a symbol of freedom and adventure. It beckons us to explore new horizons, to escape the confines of our daily routines, and to embark on new journeys. The feeling of the wind in our hair, the rumble of the engine, the ever-changing scenery – these sensations can be both exhilarating and liberating.

The road can also be a source of anxiety and uncertainty. The unknown stretches out before us, filled with both promise and peril. We may encounter unexpected obstacles, unforeseen delays, and the ever-present possibility of getting lost. This uncertainty can be both daunting and exhilarating, pushing us to step outside our comfort zones and embrace the unknown.

The road can be a mirror to our inner state. When we are feeling lost and directionless, the road may seem endless and overwhelming. When we are feeling confident and purposeful, the road may appear to be a clear and direct path towards our goals. The road, in essence, becomes a reflection of our own inner journey, with all its twists and turns, its moments of joy and despair.

The road can also be a source of connection. It brings together people from all walks of life, travelers and locals, strangers and friends. We may encounter fellow travelers at roadside diners, share stories with locals at gas stations, and forge unexpected connections with those who share our journey.

Furthermore, the road can be a symbol of our evolving relationship with the world. As technology continues to advance, our relationship with the road is also changing. We are increasingly reliant on GPS navigation, online maps, and other digital tools to guide our journeys. These technologies can both enhance and diminish our experience of the road, making our travels more efficient but potentially less adventurous.

In conclusion, the road, in its seemingly simple form, offers a profound reflection on the human experience. It's a symbol of freedom and constraint, of adventure and uncertainty, of connection and isolation. By paying attention to the road, to the journeys we undertake, and to the landscapes we traverse, we can gain valuable insights into ourselves, our relationship with the world, and the ever-changing nature of our lives

About Author

First Author:

Ajit Kumar is a compassionate and curious individual deeply invested in understanding and connecting with the world around him. He firmly believes in the inherent value of every person and strives to use his skills and talents to create a positive impact on society.

Ajit holds two Master's degrees in History, one from Nalanda University and another from IGNOU. He earned his Bachelor's degree in History from Atma Ram Sanatan Dharma College, University of Delhi. He was also selected for the prestigious Gandhi Fellowship, where he dedicated his time to various projects focused on heritage and education. His academic pursuits have been prolific, resulting in numerous research papers presented at national and international conferences and published in esteemed scholarly publications.

He has collaborated with a Post-Doctoral Fellow at Harvard University and British Library London on the transliteration of primary sources. His research has garnered significant recognition, with his papers being selected by prestigious institutions such as New York University (USA), Jawaharlal Nehru University (India), BITS Pilani, and Magadh University. Ajit's academic excellence has been further acknowledged through the prestigious Research Excellence Award 2021 and the Academic Excellence Award 2024, both bestowed upon him by the Institute of Scholars, India.

Currently, Ajit is pursuing his Ph.D. alongside maintaining a blogging website with a friend, where they explore a diverse range of topics such as inner peace, mysticism, history, and culture.

Second Author :

Rahul Verma is a compassionate individual deeply committed to fostering human connection. He actively shares his experiences to bridge gaps and build meaningful relationships with a wider audience. Seeking inner peace, he frequently explores historical and natural sites, drawing inspiration from the natural world and integrating his reflections into his understanding of human existence.

Academically, Rahul is an alumnus of prestigious Delhi University and Ambedkar University. He earned his Bachelor of Arts from Zakir Husain College, Delhi University, and his Master's in Sociology from Ambedkar University. Immersed in the vibrant intellectual atmosphere of Delhi, he developed a keen sociological understanding of the human condition.

His work challenges readers to critically examine their perceptions of reality, highlighting the profound impact of everyday experiences on individual and collective realities. Currently, Rahul serves as a PGT Sociology Teacher at Sir Padampat Singhania Education Centre, Kanpur. He is dedicated to fostering critical thinking skills in his students by integrating research perspectives into the school curriculum, preparing them for future academic endeavors. He strives to be a mentor, guiding his students to become valuable contributors to society.

###